The Tug of War

Retold by Jacquie Buttriss

Illustrated by Tania Hurt-Newton

Heinemann

Far, far away in Africa there was
a tortoise who lived with lots of
other animals.

One day Tortoise went for a walk.
She saw a hippopotamus by the river.
'I am the strongest animal in Africa,'
said Hippo, and she jumped into
the river with a big SPLASH!
'What a show-off!' said Tortoise.

Tortoise went on her way.

Then she saw an elephant by a tree.

'I am the strongest animal in Africa,'
said Elephant, and he pushed over
a tree with a big CRACK!

'What a show-off!' said Tortoise.

'So,' said Tortoise, 'Hippo and Elephant like to show off, do they? I don't like animals that show off,' she said.

So Tortoise went
back to the river
to find Hippo.

'Look at me,' called out Hippo. 'I am
so strong that I can swim up and down
all day and I don't have to stop.'

'I am strong too,' said Tortoise.

'Ha! Ha! Ha!' said Hippo.

'You can't be stronger than me.
You are only a little tortoise.'

'I **am** stronger than you,' said Tortoise.

'Come back here when the sun goes down
and I will show you how strong I am.'

Next Tortoise
went to find
Elephant.

'Look at me,' called out Elephant.
'I am so strong that I can pull up
this big tree.'

'I am strong too,' said Tortoise.

'Ha! Ha! Ha!' said Elephant.

'You can't be stronger than me.
You are only a little tortoise.'

'I **am** stronger than you,' said Tortoise.

'Come back here when the sun goes down
and I will show you how strong I am.'

That night, when the sun went down,
Hippo came back to see Tortoise.
'I will show you how strong I am.
Let's have a tug of war,' said Tortoise.
'You can't pull me over!' laughed Hippo.
'Oh yes I can,' said Tortoise. 'Here is
the rope. Pull it when I say PULL.'

So Tortoise gave
one end of the
rope to Hippo.

Then she took the other end of the
rope and walked off into the jungle.

Elephant came back to see Tortoise.

'I will show you how strong I am.

Let's have a tug of war,' said Tortoise.

'You can't pull me over!' laughed Elephant.

'Oh yes I can,' said Tortoise. 'Here is
the rope. Pull it when I say PULL.'

Tortoise gave Elephant the other end
of the rope and then she went off as
fast as she could and hid under a rock.

From there she could see Hippo by
the river and Elephant by the tree.
'PULL!' called out Tortoise.

So Hippo pulled ...

and Elephant pulled …

'I give up,' called Hippo.

'You **are** stronger than me!'

'I give up,' called Elephant.

'You **are** stronger than me!'

'Yes,' laughed Tortoise.

'I am the strongest animal in Africa.'